To William with thanks

First published in the United States 1989 by
Dial Books for Young Readers
A Division of Penguin Books USA Inc.
375 Hudson Street
New York, New York 10014

Published in Great Britain by Frances Lincoln Ltd.
Text copyright © 1989 by Matthew Sturgis
Pictures copyright © 1989 by Anne Mortimer
All rights reserved
Printed in Hong Kong
E
3 5 7 9 10 8 6 4 2

Library of Congress Cataloging in Publication Data
Sturgis, Matthew, Tosca's Christmas.
Summary: Tosca the cat fears she is going to be left
out of the celebration this Christmas, until
she is on hand to witness Santa's visit.
[1. Christmas—Fiction. 2. Cats—Fiction.
3. Santa Claus—Fiction.]
I. Mortimer, Anne, ill. II. Title.
PZ7.S9412To 1989 [E] 88-33551
ISBN 0-8037-0722-3

Tosca's Christmas

ANNE MORTIMER

STORY BY MATTHEW STURGIS

Dial Books for Young Readers ∗ *New York*

Tosca was enjoying a little nap. She was curled up snug against the cushions in a large armchair, dreaming of warm haddock.

"You can't stay there, Tosca, we've got to move that chair."

Tosca padded upstairs to find a quiet corner. She was a cat who liked her naps. Perhaps there would be a bedroom door open. There was.

All over the bed there were toys and a sea of brightly colored paper. What fun, thought Tosca, I'll gift-wrap myself. But before she could stretch her claws she was put out onto the landing.

"Go somewhere else, Tosca. I'm wrapping my presents."

Tosca wondered what was happening. She was not used to being bossed around.

There was chaos downstairs. The hallway was full of prickly holly, the kitchen thick with interesting smells. There was a large, dark plum pudding on the kitchen table and several tempting cupcakes. . . .

"No, Tosca, you can't eat one of those."

Beside the fireplace where Tosca's armchair usually stood, there was now a tall fir tree. They were all busy decorating it with glittering balls, bright streamers, and colored lights.

"Look at the Christmas tree, Tosca. Isn't Christmas exciting?"

Tosca was not excited. She sat under the tree and sulked. Tosca didn't like Christmas very much. Everyone was always too busy enjoying themselves to think of her. And nobody ever remembered to give her a present.

Tosca looked up at the glittering Christmas tree and saw an angel poised upon the very top. Would the angel grant her wish for a present? Tosca decided to ask.

She had climbed almost to the top when she felt the tree begin to wobble. It swayed for a moment, then *whoosh*, down it came with a crash of glass balls, a swish of tinsel, and a clatter of colored lights.

"Get out, Tosca! You naughty cat!"

Outside it was dark and cold. Tosca pressed her nose against the window. It looked so cozy inside. She hoped that they would let her back in. Tosca scratched at the glass, but everyone was too busy and too excited to notice.

Only the snowman was outside. And he had nothing comforting to say.

Tosca looked up at the sky and watched the stars twinkle. As she sat there, she heard the distant tinkling of bells. Then something bright and glowing passed high above her in the night sky.

As the light drew nearer and nearer, Tosca could see that it was in fact a gilded sleigh, drawn by majestic beasts with vast antlers, driven by a plump white-bearded man in a warm red suit. It was Santa Claus!

Tosca leaped to the roof as the sleigh drew to a halt.

She approached Santa Claus with a bold but friendly step and rubbed herself up against his boots.

"Hello there, pusscat," he said. "You must be cold out here. Wouldn't you be happier back inside?"

"*Purrrup, purrrup,*" said Tosca as Santa's gentle hands lifted her into the sack.

Tosca was grateful to Santa for giving her a ride down the chimney in his sack, but she was too shy to ask him whether he had brought anything for her. As Santa sat by the fire, enjoying the cupcake that had been left for him, Tosca climbed onto his large, warm lap. Santa stroked her fur and Tosca snuggled down, happy and rather drowsy. She had, after all, missed her nap. Her eyes closed and she fell fast asleep.

The next morning Tosca woke up by the fireside.

Last night's embers were still warm. From the mantle hung five stockings. One of them was much smaller than the others. It was embroidered with a large cat.

Tosca thought she must be dreaming; a stocking of her own! She tweaked her whiskers to make sure she was awake.

Then she knocked down her stocking and reached inside it. There was something quite heavy, and it was wrapped up in festive paper. Tosca tore at the wrapping with her claws, and her present came tumbling out.

It was a toy mouse all her own.

And the card read

MERRY CHRISTMAS, TOSCA